For Kate and Jane,
who always inspire me —D. M.

To all the little inspiring inventors
and scientists —J. B.

Henry Holt and Company, *Publishers since 1866*
Henry Holt® is a registered trademark of Macmillan Publishing Group, LLC
120 Broadway, New York, NY 10271 · mackids.com

Our books may be purchased in bulk for promotional, educational,
or business use. Please contact your local bookseller or the Macmillan Corporate
and Premium Sales Department at (800) 221-7945 ext. 5442 or by email at
MacmillanSpecialMarkets@macmillan.com.

Library of Congress Control Number: 2022910211

First edition, 2023
Book design by Lisa Vega
Printed in China by RR Donnelley Asia Printing Solutions Ltd.,
Dongguan City, Guangdong Province

ISBN 978-1-250-78275-5 (hardcover)
1 3 5 7 9 10 8 6 4 2

Someday, Maybe

Diana Murray

Illustrated by
Jessica Gibson

Henry Holt and Company
New York

Someday, maybe cars will fly . . .

. . . and I will be the one
who tweaks their gears and hover belts
and helps their motors run.

Someday, maybe I'll design
a house that does my chores,
like folding laundry, feeding pets,
and even mopping floors!

Someday, maybe squirmy worms
will be the new food craze—
and I will be the trendy chef
who cooks them fifty ways!

Or maybe I'll just shake my head,
say, "Earthworms? Not for me."
And open up a restaurant
where meals are all worm-free.

Someday, I might rock the stage!
I'll sing my new hit song
and program my robotic band
to play and dance along.

Or maybe I'll wear X-ray specs

to scan for broken bones.

Or send important packages
with hypersonic drones!

Or maybe when I head to work,
I'll take a space balloon . . .

. . . then transfer to a shuttle
to the first town on the moon!

Or maybe, in my dome-shaped lab,
I'll study lunar mold

and finally find a medicine
that cures the common cold.

Perhaps I'll send a rover
over sandy dunes on Mars,
or other planets, farther out,
among the twinkling stars.

I'll have a holographic crew
that does as I command,

exploring the volcanoes of
a strange, uncharted land.

Someday, maybe I'll look up
in wonder at the sky.

And maybe I'll feel homesick . . .

. . . so back to Earth I'll fly.

My family will hug me tight.

They'll be so proud of me!

And I'll keep right on dreaming . . .
of what, someday, may be.

On Our Way to Someday!

This book imagines some incredible future possibilities.
But some of what's described is already real!

Flying Cars: Flying cars have been created! But it will be a long time before they can replace regular cars. Teams of designers are working hard to make flying cars safer and less expensive.

Helpful Houses: There are already robots that can clean floors, pick up laundry, and even serve drinks. And engineers are planning "smart" homes that can do all that and more.

Yummy Worms: There are people around the world who eat mealworms, earthworms, crickets, beetles, grasshoppers, and other creepy-crawlies. Some worms and bugs are very healthy to eat and can be grown on farms.

Robot Music: Robots can do all sorts of things. Some are designed to play musical instruments. For example, one robotic band has a drummer with twenty-two arms and a guitarist with seventy-eight fingers!

X-Ray Specs: Doctors can use machines to see bones and organs inside their patients. They can also use special glasses to see veins under someone's skin. These medical technologies are getting better all the time.

Speedy Drones: The word *hypersonic* means faster than the speed of sound. That is very, very fast! The US military is already testing hypersonic drones.

Space Balloons: Have you ever seen a birthday balloon fly up to the ceiling? Or way up into the sky? Those balloons float because they're full of a gas called helium. And scientists have already created giant helium balloons that can take you floating right up to the edge of space!

Moon Town: Astronauts first walked on the moon in 1969. While we haven't started a settlement on the moon just yet, some astronauts have already lived and worked aboard the International Space Station, a spacecraft that orbits around the Earth. This helps them test how to live away from our home planet.

Mold Medicine: Penicillin, one of the most important medicines ever created, came from studying fuzzy mold, like the kind you see on old bread. And if scientists study mold up in space, where conditions are so different, maybe they can discover something new!

Space Explorers: Remote-controlled rovers and spacecraft have been sent to planets such as Mars and Jupiter. They can explore dangerous, faraway places and send useful information back to Earth.

Holograms: Holograms are like 3D images made of light. Some engineers have created holograms to do simple jobs that real people would usually do, such as greeting customers and answering questions.

There are so many things you can do someday!
Reach for the stars!
And never stop dreaming.